PREFACE

Hi—from a member of the Sugar Creek Gang!

It's just that I don't know which one I am. When I was good, I was Little Jim. When I did bad things—well, sometimes I was Bill Collins or even mischievous Poetry.

You see, I am the daughter of Paul Hutchens, and I spent many an hour listening to him read his manuscript as far as he had written it that particular day. I went along to the north woods of Minnesota, to Colorado, and to the various other places he would go to find something different for the Gang to do.

Now the years have passed—more than fifty, actually. My father is in heaven, but the Gang goes on. All thirty-six books are still in print and now are being updated for today's readers with input from my five children, who also span the decades from the '50s to the '70s.

The real Sugar Creek is in Indiana, and my father and his six brothers were the original Gang. But the idea of the books and their ministry were and are the Lord's. It is He who keeps the Gang going.

PAULINE HUTCHENS WILSON

32

SUGAR CREEK GANG

The **CEMETERY VANDALS**

Paul Hutchens

MOODY PRESS
CHICAGO

All Scripture quotations are taken from the *New American
Standard Bible,* © 1960, 1962, 1963, 1968, 1971, 1972,
1973, 1975, 1977, and 1994 by The Lockman Foundation,
La Habra, Calif. Used by permission.

Original Title: *The Worm Turns at Sugar Creek*

ISBN: 0-8024-7037-8

1 3 5 7 9 10 8 6 4 2

Printed in the United States of America

1

It hardly seems fair to blame my Saturday afternoon's unusual punishment on what a half-dozen innocent-looking fishing worms did Friday. But how else can I make anybody understand that I, Theodore Collins's first and worst son, wasn't 100 percent to blame?

Of course, I didn't realize while I was being punished—the punishment actually lasted several hours—that what was happening to me would help the gang capture a couple of prodigal sons who had been committing vandalism in and around Sugar Creek.

One of the worst things the vandals had done was to fill our spring reservoir with marsh mud. Another had been to chop a hole in the bottom of our rowboat. Also, somebody—maybe the same ornery boys—had written filthy words and drawn obscene pictures with chalk on the large, red, cylinder-shaped Sugar Creek bridge abutments.

But the very worst act of vandalism was what we discovered Thursday afternoon when we came back from our trip up into the hills, where we'd gone to look after Old Man Paddler's place.

That kind, long-whiskered old man had gone off to California for a vacation. Before he left, he had given us the responsibility of watering his house plants, filling his birdbath in the backyard patio, and—twice a week—mowing his lawn. As payment for the work, he was going to give us a whole dollar apiece, which, added up, would total six dollars, since there were that many boys in our gang.

The hole chopped in our boat stirred our tempers plenty, I tell you. And we got even madder in our minds when we saw the words on the bridge, words that weren't fit to toss into a garbage pail, and pictures that were worse to look at than a polecat is to smell.

But Thursday afternoon, when we found Old Man Paddler's wife's tombstone defaced and lying on its side in the cemetery at the top of Bumblebee Hill, that was too much to take. It just didn't seem possible that anybody in his right mind—if he had one—would want to chop a hole in a rowboat, contaminate a neighborhood's drinking water, and—worst of all—do what had been done to a dead person's gravestone! What would Old Man Paddler think, and how would he feel when he found out about it?

Maybe I'd better tell you about that Thursday afternoon right now so you'll understand why we were so boiling mad at the vandals, whoever they were.

And who were they? Were they some boys from another county who had moved into the neighborhood or somebody who already lived here? I guess maybe we all had our minds focused on the same person, but up to then we hadn't used any names in the things we had been saying—we were only getting more and more stirred up inside.

From Old Man Paddler's place, we had come past the spring, which we'd already cleaned out, and got a drink. Then we went over to the Little Jim Tree at the bottom of Bumblebee Hill to rest awhile and to talk and also to postpone a little longer having to go to our different homes, where there would be a lot of work to do. It was almost time to start the evening chores.

The Little Jim Tree was one of our favorite meeting places. We liked to lie there in the shade and remember the time Little Jim, using Big Jim's rifle, had shot and killed a fierce old mother bear. If he hadn't pulled the trigger when we yelled for him to, Little Jim might have been buried up there in the cemetery himself.

The minute we all came puffing from our fast run to the place we'd planned to meet and rest awhile, Little Jim plopped himself down on the grass at the very spot where the bear had done her dying and leaned his shoulder against the tree trunk. I think he felt kind of proud that we had named the tree after him.

The rest of us were lying in different directions, just thinking about what had been going on around the neighborhood. Still, not a one of us mentioned any name or names of anybody who might be guilty.

Big Jim, our fuzzy-mustached leader, was sitting with his knees drawn up to his chin, leaning back a little and rocking, with his fingers laced together around his shins. His face, I noticed, was set. The muscles of his jaw were tensing and untensing, the way they do when he is thinking. He was the first one to speak. "You boys remember the Battle of Bumblebee Hill?"

We remembered, all right, and several of us said so.

Then Big Jim spoke again. "Any of you remember who was the leader of the gang we had our fight with?"

That's when I knew he was thinking about the same person I was. That fight with the tough town gang that was trying to take over the whole boys' world of the Sugar Creek territory had been our fiercest battle.

The person on all our minds was John Till's oldest boy, Big Bob, whose little brother, Tom, had been in that battle, too. Tom was the one who had given me a black eye and a bashed nose.

Circus, the acrobat of our gang, had swung himself up and was sitting on the first limb of the Little Jim Tree. He said, "If Old Man Paddler gave us charge of looking after all his property while he was away, maybe we'd better have a look at his cemetery plots and at the tombstones he's got there, where his wife and two boys are buried."

It was a good idea, we thought, so we dashed

up the long grassy slope to the top. We hadn't any sooner climbed through the fence that borders the hill's rim, than Dragonfly, who was ahead of the rest of us at the time, let out a yell. "Look, everybody! Somebody's pushed over Sarah Paddler's tombstone!"

Never in my whole life had there been a feeling in my heart like what shot through me right then. It was one of the worst things I'd ever experienced. There just never was a kinder old man than Seneth Paddler, and nobody in the whole world ever had a heart that was so full of love for people, especially boys.

So it seemed I was almost as sad as if I were attending his funeral when we reached the place under the tree where, in the dappled sunlight that filtered through the branches overhead, I saw the big, tall tombstone with the name Sarah Paddler on it lying flat on the ground. Beside it was the stone that had the old man's name on it. His gravestone also had on it the date he was born. The date of his death would have to be put on some other time after the old man himself went to heaven.

Little Jim whispered in my ear in an awed voice, "Look at the hand with the finger pointing!" The carved hand with one finger pointing upward was one of the things a boy remembered. I'd seen it hundreds of times, maybe, when the stone stood straight up. The words chiseled where the wrist would have been, if there had been a wrist, said "There is rest in heaven." And there *is* for anybody who, as our Sugar Creek minister says, "trusts for his soul's salvation in the Savior and not in himself or in how good he is—or thinks he is."

Big Jim let out a groan and shook his head as if he just couldn't believe it. The grass all around the place was mashed down, and an urn that had been there with flowers growing in it was also turned over. The dirt and flowers were spilled out and scattered, and the red roses were wilted and looked like dried blood on the ground.

The right thing to do, it seemed, was to report what we'd just seen to the sheriff.

Dragonfly would have touched the stone if Poetry, our detective-minded member, hadn't stopped him. "Don't! Don't touch it! They'll want to go all over it for fingerprints!"

So we left the cemetery without touching anything and went off to make the phone call. I tell you, we were a pretty grim-faced gang as we swung out across the cemetery, climbed over the fence, hurried down the hill, passed the Little Jim Tree, and galloped on to the rail fence just across the road from my house. We crossed the road, and while the gang waited outside, I went inside and called the sheriff.

As important as making the call was, I couldn't feel proud of myself for being the one to get to do it. I was just hoping hard that the stone would be back in place and it would look the way it always had by the time Seneth Paddler came back from California.

In only about seventeen minutes, the sheriff and his deputy came driving up to our mailbox, and we all went back to the cemetery.

They went over every inch of the tombstone, several other stones around the place, and the upset urn. Near the fence they made a plaster of paris cast of somebody's shoe track.

We told him about the mud in our spring reservoir, the barnyard language we'd found and washed off the bridge abutments, and also about the hole in the bottom of our boat. We got a good looking over by the sheriff to see if any of our eyes were giving away a lie and none of them were, he decided.

"I think," he mused, as he studied us all there by the cemetery fence, where we'd been watching them make the cast of the shoe print, "you boys might be interested to know that vandals struck in town last night, too. The fountain in the park was defaced, and the water pitcher broken."

Then, to our surprise, the sheriff had every one of us lift our feet to see if any of *our* shoes had soles like the ones in the track by the fence. It was a waste of time, because every one of us was barefoot.

He winked at us then to let us know he was only joking, and we were glad he was. "The town council is offering a hundred-dollar reward," he finished, "for evidence leading to the arrest of whoever is doing this mischief."

When we were alone again, we talked for a while about the beautiful spraying fountain we'd all watched so many times in Sugar Creek

Park and the statue of the tall lady holding a stone pitcher in her right hand with water pouring out of it day and night all summer long.

Our next trip to Old Man Paddler's clapboard-roofed cabin in the hills would be Saturday. I had a feeling in my mind that we ought to go even tomorrow, but most of us had to work tomorrow, so we decided to wait.

Poetry was the last one to leave my house that afternoon. He said to me secretly before he left, "Our fishing calendar says that tomorrow is a good fishing day. Maybe we ought to go—just you and I—say, along about two o'clock at the mouth of the branch?"

"I'm not sure about that," I answered him. "Dad's gone, you know." In fact, both of our fathers were in Memory City at the agricultural convention.

"That's what I mean," he whispered back, just as my mother came out of our back door to shake a dust mop. "There won't be anybody to say we can't."

I looked at my mother's face as she shook the dust mop and said, "What do you mean, there won't be anybody?"

Mom heard my voice but maybe not what I'd just said, and she called to us, "There are two pieces of apple pie left, if anybody is hungry."

Poetry was, and pretty soon there wasn't any pie left at all.

Just as Poetry was leaving, Mom made something clear to us. "You boys being away every other afternoon this week means Bill has to work harder and faster every other day. I suppose it's that way at your house too?"

Poetry looked at me and winked, and for some reason I felt the wink was a substitute for words that were saying, "Tomorrow afternoon at two at the mouth of the branch."

Poetry was very polite around Mom when there was leftover apple pie. He thanked her with his very special company voice and shuffled off across our lawn to the gate. He opened it, went through, and then away he went, whistling down the dusty road.

It was easy to see that it wasn't going to be what anybody would call pleasant for me to work in the garden all afternoon tomorrow, which is what Mom had planned for me.

Along about five minutes to two that next afternoon, while I was working in the garden, some lively, wriggling, plump fishing worms began to be turned up by the shovel of our hand-powered garden cultivator. For some reason, I could hardly see straight for feeling there was going to be trouble of some kind—and there soon was. We were about to have one of the most exciting adventures that ever happened in the Sugar Creek territory. And this is where the worms come into this story.

Before I get into that topsy-turvy experience, though, I'd better tell you about something extraordinary that happened that night. It was something that had even more to do with the solving of our mystery than the earthworms did. What happened also set me to worrying and stirred up my anger a little more at a certain boy who lived in the neighborhood.

2

Our having reported the vandalism in our neighborhood to the sheriff didn't mean the Sugar Creek Gang had washed its hands of the problem or that we weren't interested in helping capture the guilty boys or men, whoever they were.

In fact, the hundred-dollar reward was in my mind all the while I was doing the evening chores. I flew around the barn, the chicken house, and the hog lot, getting Dad's work done as well as my own.

In the haymow, throwing down alfalfa for the cows, I stopped hurrying, though. I climbed up on the eight-by-ten-inch beam that stretches all the way across the barn, and with as oratorical a voice as I could, I recited the Gettysburg Address, winding up with an important change in the words, saying, "That government of the Sugar Creek Gang, by the Sugar Creek Gang, and for the Sugar Creek Gang shall not perish from the territory!"

My voice sounded a little lower in pitch than it used to, I thought. I wondered if maybe I was getting old enough to have what people call a "voice change." If it was changing, that meant that pretty soon I might be old enough to shave.

It seemed also that the last words of the address—the ones I had altered—were arrows with sharp barbs on each one, and that I was shooting them fast and straight at any vandals that might be trying to take over and run the territory to suit themselves. "If I ever get a chance to strike that thing, I'll strike it hard!" I repeated to myself, remembering something Abraham Lincoln had once said about slavery.

Thinking that, I jumped off the beam into the hay, swept up the three-tine pitchfork, and whirled into throwing down the hay. I was thinking, *No wonder Poetry wants to go fishing tomorrow. He's got something to tell me about who is doing the malicious mischief. Poetry is the best detective in the whole Sugar Creek Gang. Maybe if I meet him tomorrow at the month of the branch at two o'clock—*

That was as far as I got to think about that right then, because I heard a woman's high-pitched voice calling from the house. It was my mother, wanting me to come quick about something.

I did come quick and, as I got close to the house, was surprised at the wonderful odor coming from the kitchen. It was almost supper time, but generally I didn't get called until the last minute.

"Get the picnic basket," Mom ordered me. "We'll have to hurry now to get there in time."

"Get where in time for what?" I asked as I started toward the west room just off the kitchen. The top shelf of the linen closet was

where we kept the large round wicker bask[ ]
the Collins family always used when they went
on a picnic.

She startled me by saying, "To the Tills'.
Mrs. Till's in bed sick, and tonight's our turn to
furnish the dinner."

I was a little confused in my mind. I felt hot
tempered at Bob Till, and now my mother said
we were going over to their house to take his
mother a casserole of food that smelled good
enough for us to have for our own supper!

But in a little while, Mom and Charlotte
Ann and I were in the car. Mom was driving,
and I was in the backseat with the picnic basket,
baby-sitting—and wrestling—with my sometimes-
cute little sister to keep her from standing up
on the seat or walking on the picnic basket.

"How sick is Mrs. Till?" I asked Mom. She
spent more time in our house than I did and
talked on the telephone about different things
and people.

Mom's voice came back over her shoulder
above the sound of the car engine. "She may
have to have an operation. The doctor was
there this morning. That's why the neighborhood women are taking over. We may have to
drive her to the hospital ourselves."

"Where's old Hook-nose?" I asked. "Can't
he take her?"

Mom said something sharp. But we had just
reached the Sugar Creek bridge, and the car
wheels were making the floorboards rattle. The
vibration was shaking the rafters. I could hardly

hear what she was saying. But then she said, "John Till is in Valparaiso on a road job, and Tom is with him. They left just yesterday, and it'd be a shame to call him home so soon—not when he hasn't had work for over a month."

We were across the bridge now, but I could tell by Mom's face in the rearview mirror that she didn't want me *ever* again to call John Till "old Hook-nose." It wasn't polite. "Hook-nose," as you maybe know, is the name our gang had called him for several years when he was such a wicked father and before he had been saved from drowning. Boy, had that been a spine-tingling adventure!

Up to now, his son Bob was just as ornery a boy as he had ever been. Of that I was very sure. And he proved he was still the same when Mom and Charlotte Ann and I went into their old, unpainted, but surprisingly clean house to take Mrs. Till her supper.

It took Mom only a few minutes to get Mrs. Till propped up on pillows and to carry her a tray of hot beef and noodles, a cool green salad, and other tasty-looking food.

Bob, who had been in the house when we came, was quickly out the back door. He was nowhere around while we sat and visited a little with his mother.

"I know I need an operation," Mrs. Till said, "but you know how it is—you just keep putting it off. And with John out of work and all . . ."

Once I heard a sound at the kitchen door

and saw a boy's mussed-up head of hair and a pair of eyes peeking at us. But it was only for a second. Then he was gone again, and I heard a door slam in another part of the house.

"Bob's timid about meeting people," his mother apologized. "But he's been good to me since John left, washing the dishes, keeping plenty of firewood in the box . . ."

I wasn't sure I wanted to hear anybody say Bob had been kind to his mother, not when he could do such terrible things as it seemed he had been doing around our neighborhood.

Also, I wasn't sure it was timidity that kept him out of the room while we were there.

I got one of the biggest surprises of my life right about then—one that worried me a little.

While my mother was holding a straw for Mrs. Till to take a sip of the cold water I'd just pumped from their wooden-handled pump, Mom asked, "Has our pastor called on you since you've been down?"

"Not yet," Mrs. Till answered and sighed as if she was having a little trouble getting enough fresh air. It *was* stuffy in the room—with the sun shining its good-bye to the territory through a long torn place in the green window blind. *We ought to be going soon,* I thought, *so there'll be more air for one person to breathe.*

Then, as if Mrs. Till didn't want anybody to be blamed, especially our minister, she added, "He phoned this morning to tell me he was praying. He had a funeral this afternoon at his former church in Placerville. He's been so kind to us."

"Maybe, dear," Mom said, "you'd like to hear a little something from the Book?"

Bob Till's mother said yes and pointed to the table beside her bed where her half-worn-out Bible lay.

My thoughtful mother opened the Bible to a place in one of the psalms and was about to read. That's when I got my surprise.

"Run out and see if Bob would like to come in," Mrs. Till said to me.

Imagine that! With all the anger in my heart toward Bob Till, *I* was expected to go out and ask him to come in to hear my mother read a psalm from the Bible?

But I had to go, and I did go, and I got a short answer from Big Bob Till. He was standing at the woodpile with an ax in his hand, only waiting till I got through asking him, so that he could start splitting wood again.

He was too busy, he said. He had to get the firewood split before dark.

On the way back to the house door, I had in my mind's eye not a boy with an ax splitting wood but that same ax being raised in the humid air near the old swimming hole and coming down *ker-wham* into the bottom of somebody's rowboat!

Mom read the psalm, and then Mrs. Till said, "I'm sure Pastor Johnson would be pleased to have you pray too."

And then came the rest of the surprise. My

own mother, who, it seemed, ought to know better, asked me, Bill Collins—in my bad mood—to pray the way a minister was supposed to pray at somebody's bedside!

I had to do it—and I did it—wishing even while I was saying the words that I was as sincere as maybe I sounded. I could hardly hear myself anyway, on account of from the backyard there was the *chop—chop—chop—chop—chop* of a powerful-muscled boy using an ax.

It didn't seem right for me to pray while feeling like that, so on the way home, with nobody knowing what I was doing except Theodore Collins's own ornery son, I asked God's forgiveness and felt a little better even before we had reached the bridge.

There wasn't any use to ask Mom's forgiveness. Right that second she was saying, "I was so proud of you, Bill. That was such a nice prayer—and so comforting. Did you notice the tears in her eyes when you finished?"

I swallowed a lump in my throat and didn't answer.

She stepped on the brake, then turned off the motor. "Let's listen awhile," she said.

"To what?" I asked but needn't have, because from the marsh below us on the west came one of the prettiest sounds a boy ever hears around Sugar Creek—frogs trilling and redwing blackbirds calling to each other from the willows.

"I used to come here often when I was a girl," Mom said, "and I just wanted to relive some of the memories." Then she added, "When you're as old as I am, you'll have memories like this, too. And you'll love them. They'll make drab days easier to take. It's the little things that pleased you as a boy that will make rainbows out of your stormy times."

I didn't really understand what she was trying to tell me, but I could tell it made her feel happy inside to hear birds singing and frogs trilling and to just sit in the twilight and look at a sunset.

But her memories got interrupted then, and she had to leave her peaceful past for the stormy present to hurry on home and get a fussy Charlotte Ann her supper. We had stayed at the Tills' quite a lot longer than we had planned to.

Well, as I mentioned in the first chapter of this story, about five minutes to two the next day my plow began to turn up long, slender worms with tapering ends.

It didn't seem important right then that my father was always glad there were a lot of earthworms in our garden. He said they helped keep the soil loose and that, when they got through digesting all the dirt they could eat every day, they brought the part they couldn't digest to the surface, which is very good for a garden. What did seem important right then was that an earthworm could go down deep in the water and bring a sunfish or a bass to the surface and that a boy could eat and digest the fish. Very important, in fact.

Grunt and groan and sweat and wish I could go fishing—the hardest part about working was wanting to do something else. A sentence I'd read somewhere was following me back and forth across the garden, as I pushed the lazy little one-wheeled, one-shoveled garden cultivator along between the rows of lettuce. It kept repeating itself in my mind: *Nothing is work unless you'd rather be doing something else . . . Nothing is work unless . . .*

"I, Bill Collins, Theodore Collins's first and worst son, would rather be doing something else. Therefore what I am doing right now is work—hard work!" I complained to myself.

It took me almost thirteen tiring minutes before I finished the black-seeded Simpson lettuce and had started to cultivate the Ebenezer onions. Ebenezer was Mom's favorite variety of onions, maybe because the name was a Bible name and meant "Up to now, the Lord has helped us."

But *now* was two o'clock, and that was worrying me. Mom had gone to town for groceries and wouldn't be home for quite a while, she had told me. She hadn't actually said I *couldn't* go fishing.

As I have just said, I had the black-seeded Simpson lettuce all cultivated and had started on the Ebenezer onions when I noticed the long, very fat, squirming, shining, lively fishing worms being turned up by my hand-plow shovel.

I don't know how it happened—or maybe I do—but almost before I got to the end of the row I was cultivating, all of a sudden it looked as if there weren't more than twenty minutes of work left and I'd be done. Why, I could get to the mouth of the branch, catch all the fish that would bite, and still be home and going back and forth between the last few rows of Golden Bantam by the time our car came driving in past "Theodore Collins" on our mailbox!

3

I wouldn't actually be disobeying my mother, and I wouldn't be disappointing my almost-best friend, Leslie "Poetry" Thompson, if I went fishing for just a little while, I thought. "You'll be killing two birds with one stone," I said, quoting an old proverb.

The one-wheeled cultivator was leaning against the gate, where I could get it in a hurry when I came back with maybe more fish than I had ever caught in my life before in one afternoon—if Poetry's almanac was right. Why, there might not even be another day that whole summer when the almanac would say it was such a good fishing day!

The only thing was that time seems to fly a lot faster when a boy is lying in the shade at the mouth of the branch, catching one fish after another, than it does when that same boy is sweating back and forth between long, dusty hot rows of Ebenezer onions.

It was nearly four o'clock before I knew it. But even then I couldn't go home. Poetry had it in his mind that we ought to go to the Sugar Creek bridge again to see if there'd been any more vandalism—which we did, and there hadn't been.

From the bridge, we went back to where we

had set our poles, and it took me quite a while longer to land the whopper of a catfish that had swallowed my hook while I was gone and had twisted my line around a sunken tree branch on the bottom.

It was a little out of the way to go past the sycamore tree and the mouth of the cave—out of the way if you were going to my house but not if you were going to Poetry's.

"We might have a leftover piece of cherry pie," he tempted me. "That way my mother could pay back your mother for yesterday's apple pie."

Any boy knows it is always good to pay back what you borrow, so it did seem I ought to help Poetry's mother get even with my mother that way.

When we came to the cave, we stood for a minute, studying its strong, extraheavy new door. Old Man Paddler had put it there before he left for California.

Tomorrow we'd all be standing there waiting for Big Jim to unlock the door with the key the old man had left with him. Then we'd follow the long, winding, narrow, uphill underground passage all the way to the cellar door of the old man's cabin, unlock that door, and, after climbing up a short stairway to the trapdoor, be inside the very homelike place we all liked so well.

That cave certainly made a fine shortcut for us and also for the old man when he was in a hurry to get from his place to the neighborhood where we all lived or from our neighbor-hood to his own.

"A vandal would have a hard time breaking down a door like that," I said, "but I suppose he could chop his way in with an ax, if he was mean enough to."

"Any boy who would chop through the bottom of a rowboat would be that mean," was Poetry's set-faced answer. The way he said it set my own temper on edge again against whoever was doing all the malicious mischief.

It certainly felt fine that there wasn't one of the Sugar Creek Gang who would want to destroy anybody else's property. It also felt good to be trusted by Old Man Paddler to look after his place for him.

That kind old man had even showed us his secret hiding place for the spare key to the cave.

Poetry and I moseyed over to the hollow sycamore tree. And just to help myself feel a little more proud that we could be trusted, I reached my arm in, felt around behind a shelf of dead wood, and brought out the secret key on its little chain.

In that fleeting second my mind unwrapped the memory I had in it of the time I'd gotten stuck inside that tree. That's in a story called *Western Adventure*. I had had to stay there until way into the night before I could get out and had been as badly scared as I'd ever been in my life.

Holding and looking at the key we had

been trusted with made me feel as fine as I do when I look at the little bankbook I have at home, which shows how much money I have saved out of my allowance. It certainly makes a boy feel rich to be trusted like that.

I was holding the key with my left hand when I all of a sudden saw my wristwatch. It told me that it was past time to get started on the run for the Collins front gate and get myself out into the garden with the Ebenezer onions before Mom came home—which I just might not be able to do.

Well, the Collins family had six sunfish and one catfish for supper that night. Mom had been home a long time, and for some reason I didn't get a single bite of her freshly baked custard pie. Also, I got to go to bed as soon as the after-supper chores were finished. Worst of all, I wasn't going to get to go with the gang next day to help them look after Old Man Paddler's place in the hills.

I think it hurt my mother's tender heart not to let me go, but after she decided something, there wasn't any use to try to get her to change her mind. It wasn't good for a boy for a mother to do that, she had told me.

Lying upstairs in bed like the boy in Robert Louis Stevenson's poem who "had to go to bed by day," I thought about some advice the old man had given us just before he left for California: "You boys have proved that you can be trusted, and I know that when I get back my flowers won't be wilted, the grass will be cut, and the birds will be having the time of their lives in the birdbath out on the patio. One thing I want you to be very sure about is always to lock the doors when you leave. An unlocked door, boys, is an invitation to thieves."

I had been a little surprised at what he said next, but it seemed he was right. He was a very wise old man and knew the Bible almost by heart. He said, "One of the Ten Commandments is 'You shall not steal.' I've always figured that since it is wrong to steal, it's also wrong for us to make it easy for anybody else to do it. That's why, whenever you leave home, it's wise to lock the doors. And never leave your car unlocked or the keys in the ignition."

There was a rustling of the leaves of the ivy vine that grew across the corner of the window next to my bed. From the plum tree, a father robin was whooping it up. I thought he might be saying that it had been a wonderful day and for his robin wife to go to sleep without a worry in the world because he was around to look after her.

Robins, I thought sadly, *don't have any parents to obey, and if they want to take off anywhere for a trip across the sky, they can do it.*

I was feeling pretty sorry for myself, yet I knew there wasn't any use licking my sore feelings like a hound that's been in a fight with a coon. When a red-haired only-son's parents come to what Mom that very afternoon called "the end of my patience rope" for neglecting his garden work and going fishing instead of doing it, there isn't anything that sad son can do except take his punishment.

The worst thing about it, I thought with a sigh, was that I couldn't just take my punishment and get it over with because my father wasn't home. If he had been home, I might have gotten it over in a hurry.

But he wasn't home and wouldn't be until after the trip to Old Man Paddler's cabin tomorrow would be some kind of history. If he had been home, I could have had a good old-fashioned switching in the woodshed, and then I could have had custard pie for dessert, an hour or more twilight fun, and gone to bed by night like any other human being that wasn't a baby.

But my tenderhearted mother didn't like to punish her son by a beech switch in a wood-shed. It hadn't been her way of doing it for quite a while because of something she had read in a book she had borrowed at the library.

In that book was a chapter called "Discipline Through Affection," and in that chapter was a paragraph with a heading called "To Spank or Not to Spank." I had sort of accidentally read that chapter myself, and the very last sentence of it was probably what Mom had especially liked. It ran something like this: "The best that can be said for spanking is that it sometimes clears the air."

Dad had disagreed with the library book because of something *he'd* read in the newspaper that comes to our house. For some reason, I had read that same article, which had the very interesting title "Spanking's Still a Good Teacher."

In spite of my sad feeling, I must have gone to sleep, because all of a sudden it was morning. The father robin was yelling what a wonderful day it was with nothing to do, our old red rooster was bragging with his *cock-a-doodle-do* that he was the most important chicken in the flock, and a slant of sunlight was lying across the windowsill of my room—also with nothing to do.

The morning wasn't so bad, and for lunch at noon I got to eat an extralarge piece of yesterday's custard pie. My mother's face wasn't sad anymore, but she was very busy getting ready for a committee meeting of some kind at the Thompsons'.

I was going to get to have my humane punishment all by myself. I was to be my own boss while I finished yesterday's garden work. The punishment was finishing the Ebenezer onions, weeding the Golden Bantam sweet corn, hoeing the Yellow Cherry tomatoes, and thinning out the Scarlet Globe radishes.

"Can't I even rest a little while between the rows of Golden Bantam?" I asked just before Mom drove away, and she surprised me with, "You be your own boss."

I was standing beside the car door. Mom was under the steering wheel. Charlotte Ann was on the seat beside her, cranky fussy and whining with the heat and from needing to go to bed by day and not wanting to. She would have to when they got to the Thompsons'.

"If your conscience tells you to rest a little now and then," Mom finished, "that's up to you. It is a very hot afternoon."

Charlotte Ann was making it hard for Mom and me to hear each other. Because I wanted to have a better feeling between myself and the most wonderful mother there ever was, I ordered my little sister to pipe down, saying, "What are *you* so cranky about? You're not being punished for anything!"

But it was the wrong thing to say and maybe not even right to think, because Charlotte Ann was not only my ornery little sister, she was also Mom's only baby girl. My mother's tone of voice was a little sharper than she usually uses on me when she answered, "She doesn't know any better. She's just cranky-sleepy. She's used to her nap this time of day."

Still trying to say something that would make a better feeling between us, I began, "Be sure not to leave the keys in the ignition when you're in the house having your committee meeting, Old Man Paddler says."

Mom for some reason didn't seem to realize that I was trying to prove to her I wasn't such a thoughtless boy after all. She interrupted me with, "Mrs. Thompson doesn't know how to drive, and there's not likely to be a woman there who would want to steal a car."

She did smile though, to show me she still liked me in spite of me, and she started the car.

In a few seconds she was gone, driving through the gate out onto the road and almost speeding to get to the Thompsons' as soon as she could.

I was left to go out into the garden to be my own boss for a while.

As I watched the trail of whitish brown dust boiling up behind the car and being carried by the lazy afternoon breeze in the direction of the papaw trees in the woods, I realized that the feeling between Mom and me was still not very good. And it wouldn't be until I had yesterday's garden work finished.

Now, will you tell me how in the world a boy can be his own boss and make himself do what he, the boss, doesn't want to do in the first place?

Anyway, Mom hadn't been gone more than a few minutes and I had just finished one row of Ebenezer onions when I, the boss, said to myself, "All right, son, you've been working pretty hard, and you're thirsty. Go get yourself a drink."

"Yes sir," I said to myself.

Leaning the cultivator against the garden gate, I made my tired way to the iron pitcher pump at the end of the board walk that runs back and forth between the pump and the house. I pumped a few sad, squeaking strokes and drank half a cupful of the cool, clean water that gushed out the pump's pitcher-shaped spout. Then I tossed the other half over and across the top of the iron kettle, where it landed in a puddle and scattered thirteen or more thirsty yellow butterflies in that many fluttering directions.

Then I pumped a pail of water and walked it around to the west side of the house to pour it into the trough that circles the little two-foot-tall blue spruce we'd set out there just last week, halfway between the two cherry trees at the end of the row of hollyhocks.

That very pretty, symmetrical blue spruce tree was my birthday present to my mother— since I'm the best son she ever had, and also the worst, as Pop sometimes says. I am also their only son.

I ordered me to stop and admire that happy little tree, and for a few seconds I felt proud of myself for planning the present for Mom. With the help of the gang, we had managed, in spite of a thunderstormy afternoon, to get it dug and balled and set out right here where she could see it every time she looked out the west window. We had actually brought the tree home from Old Man Paddler's place in the hills in a *helicopter*.

While I was still standing and admiring the tree, thinking about how much I liked my brownish gray haired mother and how she always tried to keep me from being punished in a noisy way, I began to feel sadder than ever.

"I never saw anybody with such a tender heart," I said to myself and to the little tree, remembering it was right at this very spot one day that Mom had accidentally stepped on a baby chicken and had felt sad all day because of it. At another time a bluebird had come flying as fast as a baseball off a boy's bat and whammed into the west window and killed itself. Mom wouldn't even let our old black-and-white cat have the bird for supper but had me bury it out in the garden.

It certainly didn't feel good to think that by neglecting my work and thoughtlessly going fishing, I had stepped on Mom's heart like a careless boy stepping on a fluffy little chicken.

Thinking that, I began to feel bad inside because of all the other sad thoughts that were making a crow's nest in my already sad mind.

And that's when all of a sudden I spied, at the base of the spruce tree, a single dogtooth violet growing in the ball of dirt we'd brought the tree's roots in. And that is one of the prettiest yellow flowers that grows around Sugar Creek. Dragonfly, the pop-eyed member of our gang, calls the dogtooth violet a fawn lily. Little Jim calls it a trout lily. And Circus calls it a yellow adder's tongue. All the names are local names for the same flower.

Surprised, I stood and stared at the six-tongued yellow flower and at the two mottled green and purple white leaves its stem seemed to be growing out of. Hardly knowing what I was doing, I heard myself mumbling a poem I'd had to memorize at school. It was written by somebody called Wordsworth, I remembered.

And because our rain barrel was not more than ten feet behind me at the corner of the house, I ordered me to go over to it, stick my head inside, and yell the poem down into it just to hear the hollow sound my voice would make:

"I wandered lonely as a cloud
  That floats on high o'er vales and hills,
  When all at once I saw a crowd,
  A host, of golden daffodils;
  Beside the lake, beneath the trees,
  Fluttering and dancing in the breeze."

My head was still in the barrel when I got to the end of the first stanza. There was something else in the barrel, too. There were fifteen or twenty little wrigglers in the water, which I knew were mosquitoes in the larva stage.

The third stanza of the poem, I remembered, told that seeing the "crowd" of golden daffodils made the poet forget how lonely and unhappy he was.

I lifted my head out of the barrel and, from looking at the crowd of baby mosquitoes, went back to the baby spruce tree and stood staring down at the six-parted lemon yellow flower and its dappled, lance-shaped leaves. But it didn't do anything for me except make me feel worse about my not getting to go to Old Man Paddler's with the gang.

I kept on standing and looking and quoting to myself the part of the poem where Wordsworth says that sometimes, when he is lying on a couch resting, all of a sudden he sees the daffodils with his inner eye, and in a flash his sad heart is full and running over with what he calls "pleasure."

It sounded so encouraging that I quoted it to the crowd of wrigglers in the barrel, and for a few seconds I actually felt better because of the echoes my voice made. Hollering down a rain barrel is something any boy likes to do anyway.

"For oft, when on my couch I lie
   In vacant or in pensive mood,
   They flash upon that inward eye
   Which is the bliss of solitude;
   And then my heart with pleasure fills,
   And dances with the daffodils."

The wrigglers kept on wriggling, and my mind kept on feeling mostly sad, so I gave up, took a long last look at the dogtooth violet, and ordered myself into the house. There, in as vacant and pensive a mood as I could imagine myself into, I lay down on the couch, shut my eyes, and gave the dogtooth violet a chance to flash upon my inner eye.

After waiting five or maybe six or seven minutes, I realized there wasn't any use to pretend. My name was William Collins, not William Wordsworth.

What did flash upon my inner eye was a beech switch stretched across the two tenpenny nails driven into the woodshed wall above the workbench. My inner ear kept hearing voices down along the creek, laughing, shouting, and tossing wisecracks, where six boys fluttered and danced and leapfrogged in the breeze.

Of course, there wouldn't be six, but only five. Only five . . . only five . . . only five . . . .

There just had to be something I could do to get the sad feeling out of my heart.

4

My outer eyes roved around the room, resting first on one thing and then another. There was the organ in the corner, and the hymnbook on the rack was opened to one of Mom's favorite hymns. Even from as far away as I was at the time, I could see it was "What a Friend We Have in Jesus." I'd heard her sing that song many times, pumping the organ, and following the notes with her soprano voice.

Thinking that with my mind and hearing Mom's voice with my inner ear made me feel even worse. I remembered that late yesterday afternoon when I had come back from my fishing trip with the six sunfish and one ugly catfish, my wonderful mother hadn't even scolded me. "Scolding sharply," the library book had said, "is an inhumane way of punishing. It cuts long, ragged slashes in the child's heart."

"If you get them cleaned in a hurry," she had said to me, "we'll have them for supper."

It wasn't the thing she said or the way she said it that hurt but *where* she was when she said it. She was out in the garden pushing the one-wheeled, two-handled cultivator back and forth between the long rows of Ebenezer onions!

I guess maybe I'll never again enjoy the wonderful taste of sunfish and catfish rolled in cornmeal and fried in butter till they are a golden brown.

My eyes rested on several other things in the room. One of them was the mantel on the north wall between the window and the front door. The mirror standing on the mantel had a triangular piece of glass missing out of the lower lefthand corner. That mirror had been broken by my parents' only son one day when he'd lost his temper about something and tossed an ash walking stick he'd brought into the house with a *ker-wham* onto the living-room floor. The stick had bounced from the floor to the corner of the mirror and back to the floor again. The mirror had never had new glass put in, so that ever since, when I looked at my outer self in it, I also saw a hot-tempered boy's inner self.

By the mantel was the library table, and on it lay Mom's brown-leather Bible.

All of a sudden it seemed I ought to get up and go over to the Bible and open it to see if I could find anything in it about how a boy could be a better boy and—if he was his own boss—make himself behave himself.

I got a fine surprise when I did do what it had seemed I ought to do, though what I read didn't make me happy at first. In fact, it made me feel even worse than Wordsworth had been feeling while he wandered lonely as a cloud. The marked verse in the New Testament part of the Bible where Mom had put a bookmark said, "If we confess our sins, He is faithful and righteous to forgive us our sins and to cleanse us from all unrighteousness."

It came to me then, like a streak of lightning in a dark thundercloud, that I, Bill Collins, ought to admit to my mother and to the One whose book the Bible was, that I had actually done more than neglect my work and disobey my parents. I had honest-to-goodness-for-sure sinned.

What I needed to do was to come straight out and say so to God—and right now!

I walked over to the big chair near the bedroom door, where I'd seen Mom on her knees quite a few times with Dad beside her, and down I went.

With my eyes shut, I said, "What I did yesterday was worse than disobedience. It was a sin against You, and I would like to have my heart washed, like it says."

And the strangest thing flashed on my inner eye right then. I saw a boy I knew pretty well—because his shadow goes in and out with me all the time—come storming into the living room with a hot temper and slam an ash walking stick down onto the floor. With my inner ear I could almost hear the breaking of the mirror. The next thing I knew I was saying out loud, "And the mirror I broke. I guess I never did confess that, either. If that sin is still buried in a corner of my heart somewhere, I'd like to have it cleaned out, too."

In a flash, I was finished with my prayer and off my knees and feeling fine. Then I ran out of the living room through the kitchen and out-doors onto the board walk like a streak of two-legged lightning on my way to the garden. Inside I was feeling as light as a floating feather, and it didn't seem to matter whether I got to go with the gang on its Saturday afternoon hike to Old Man Paddler's cabin or not.

That is, it didn't seem to matter until I'd finished the Golden Bantam sweet corn and was getting another drink from the iron pitch-er pump's pitcher-shaped spout, watching the yellow butterflies lazying their way back to their water puddle again.

I was still feeling fine inside at the time. I could have danced with a host of beech switch-es like the one lying across the two tenpenny nails above the workbench in the woodshed. And that's when the party-line phone rang in the house, two extralong longs and a very short short.

"Our number!" I, the boss, exclaimed to me. "You answer it, Son, and see who it is. Tell 'em I'm busy for the afternoon—tied up until four o'clock. After that I can talk or have com-pany."

I was in the house, letting the door slam behind me, and all the way through the kitchen and into the living room before I had finished giving myself the orders.

"Hello," I said in a businesslike voice. "Bill Collins's residence speaking!" I did sound very dignified, I thought, and was proud of my voice, which, beginning a few months ago, had almost begun to change a little the way a boy's voice is supposed to do when he gets old enough.

But the ducklike voice on the other end of the party line wasn't dignified. Instead it was very excited. It was good old Poetry himself, the roundest member of our gang. Leslie "Poetry" Thompson was calling from Old Man Paddler's cabin. He was half shouting as he told me, "Drop everything and run like a deer to the cave and lock the door! We left it wide open when we came up so we could see our way better—we only had one flashlight!"

What Poetry was yelling for me to do didn't make sense until he managed to get across to my vacant mind that they had found some vandals in the cabin!

"They'd smashed things up, knocked over the window planter and the old man's dish cabinet. One of them's got his radio, and they're both down in the cave! They went storming down the stairs and into the cellar, and they're in the cave right now! *Hurry up!*" Poetry wound up yelling!

"OK! OK!" I shouted back, and in a fleeting flash I was pedaling furiously down the road on my bike on the way to the sycamore tree to get the spare key. Then I would fly to the big wooden door of the cave and lock it before the vandals could get there and get out.

I knew it was quite a long way from the old man's cellar through the cave to its mouth, and it'd take them quite a while if they had to make it in the dark without a flashlight. But if they *had* a flashlight, even with the narrow places and the up-and-down places and the one slippery place, they might easily beat me in what was maybe one of the most important races I'd ever run in my half-long life.

If I'd been watching more carefully instead of thinking so worriedly, maybe I'd have missed running over that sharp rock in the road and my front bike tire wouldn't all of a sudden have gone *swoosh . . . hissssss!* Its flat sides began to scrape, and I had to slam on my brakes, swing myself off, push the bike out to the side of the road, and lean it any old way it happened to land against the trunk of a maple tree.

But I couldn't let a flat tire keep me from getting to the cave before some powerful-muscled vandals came storming out like bats out of a cavern.

Hurry—hurry—hurry. My bare feet flew down the road to the branch bridge and across it. I took a side glance to the left toward Poetry's house several hundred yards away and saw the Collins family car parked in their driveway not far from the side door. I hoped Mom wouldn't be sitting near any of the windows of the big house and see me. Her afternoon's peace and quiet would be upset, if it wasn't already upset by Charlotte Ann's cranky-sleepy fussing.

In another second I had dived down the bank on the other side of the branch and was following it to Sugar Creek. The surface of the creek itself was as quiet as Wordsworth on a couch. Not a ripple was dancing on it. It was, in fact, as smooth as glass and as clear as a living-room mirror.

Over brush piles and around fallen logs, through narrow places where the path was bordered by weeds as high as a man's head, I went on and on and still on, wondering, worrying, hoping. Also, even though what I was doing was right, it still seemed something was chasing me, something like a boy's shadow reminding him that he had left an unfinished garden somewhere in another world.

I was within maybe a hundred feet of the sycamore tree now, and I could see the wide-open door.

Maybe, as I dashed past on my way to the hollow tree to get the key, I could quick slam the door shut and make it darker inside and harder for the vandals to see their way. That would slow them down—unless they had already come out and were already gone in some direction or other.

Puff . . . puff . . . pant . . . pant. My lungs were hurting from working so hard to keep me in enough breath.

It seemed all the time that I was an even better boy than I knew I was, because I not only wanted to help bring the vandals to justice, but I also wanted to help the gang earn the reward money.

One thought was bothering me, though. Was one of the boys Big Bob Till, whose mother was sick in bed and needed an operation? And if

Bob was one of the culprits, would our catching him be like walking on his mother's heart?

I was within a few feet of the cave door. And then—in another few seconds—I was there.

Slam! The door went shut with a bang, and I knew it would be as dark inside as a night without any moon or stars.

It was on to the sycamore tree. I was hardly able to see for the sweat in my eyes and my mussed-up hair.

And then, all of painful sudden I was down, with my right big toe hurting as though a horse had stepped on it. Suddenly I had a headache from striking my head on the same tree root I had already stubbed my toe on.

I got up again and limped on to the tree. I had my arm inside and my fingers on the key, and that's when I heard voices. I heard the big wooden door of the cave open. I also saw it swing wide and boys come rushing out. I was so dizzy from the pain in my toe and foot and head that it seemed there were maybe even four or five boys, but I couldn't tell.

One thing my muddled mind let me know was that it was too late to lock the door. The trap we were trying to set had been sprung, and the "rats" had gotten away.

One thing I *could* do, and that I started to do, refusing to let my aching head and my bruised big toe stop me. I could give chase to see which way whoever I was chasing would go, and I could also get to the Thompsons' house and phone the sheriff.

And then I was on my kind of wobbly feet and running. I told myself I just had to keep them in sight.

Well, any boy knows that whenever he gets hurt, there is first of all a fierce, fast rush of pain to the place where he gets hurt. Then, a very few seconds later, if his injury is not serious, a sort of hot feeling comes into the place and he feels better.

I hadn't been running long when I heard a voice behind me, and then another and another. It was the good old Sugar Creek Gang itself, out of the cave and giving chase with me—all of us like six hounds on a hot coon trail.

In fact, Circus, whose father is a hunter and owns and hunts at night with a true bluetick hound and a purebred Black and Tan, let out a long, wailing bawl as if he was a hound himself. His high-pitched, trembling bawl was so much like old Black and Tan's that it almost seemed we all were actually on a hot coon chase.

"They're heading for our barnyard!" Poetry cried behind us. "What're they running toward where anybody lives for?"

What *were* they heading for, anyway? I wondered. I now managed to see through the thicket of bushes ahead of us that there were *two* husky-looking teenage boys—not four or five. They were dressed in dark jeans and gray T-shirts.

"Let's head 'em off!" Circus cried and shot out ahead of the rest of us toward the Thompsons' toolshed. The swiftest runner of the gang was going like a curly-headed arrow now and gaining fast.

Dragonfly, panting and wheezing a little on account of his asthma, cried out, "There th–th–there th–th–they g–g–o!"

And there they did go, like boys in a hundred-yard dash in a track meet, not toward the toolshed now but toward the heavy shrubbery that fenced in the Thompsons' big grassy lawn —also straight toward Theodore Collins's car, parked in the driveway near the Thompsons' side door.

Well, a brain-whirling fear swept into my mind then, and a frightening question thundered itself at me: *What if Mom left the key in the ignition?*

In seconds, my question would be answered. One of the rough boys we'd been chasing—the one who was carrying Old Man Paddler's radio —swung past the Thompsons' spirea hedge and scooted like a streak for the car door. The larger boy circled the car. Then two doors opened and banged shut again in a noisy hurry.

And that's when my question was answered. Mom *had* left our key in the ignition! The engine leaped into life, and as quick as a cat starting in a fast race toward a tree to get away from a chasing dog, the Collins family car was gone. And I was startled to remember that on the key ring with the ignition key were several others. One of them was the key to our house!

First, the car shot backward a few feet, stopped with a screeching of brakes, and then it was off toward the Thompsons' red barn, following their circular drive.

Where on earth were they going?

I needn't have wondered. A second later, the car was cutting a wide circle and heading back again straight toward where six boys were standing and staring.

"Out of the way!" Big Jim cried to us.

Six boys leaped aside just in time as our car swooshed past us toward the open gate, slowed down, then shot forward and through. It swung onto the road and went storming down the hill toward the branch bridge.

I was on the ground at the side of the Thompsons' driveway, where I'd landed in my headlong dive for safety, when I heard the house door open and the excited, worried voice of my mother.

She came rushing out to where the car had been. "Charlotte Ann!" she exclaimed. "She was asleep in the backseat!"

5

Now *what* do you do at a time like that? There we were—six upset boys, startled half out of what few wits we had but glad to be alive and unhurt, and maybe the finest mother there ever was in the whole world, worried half to death because the stolen car had her little girl asleep in the backseat. And that car, I could tell from the wake of boiling dust it was making as it roared up the hill on the other side of the branch bridge, was going maybe seventy miles an hour with a lunatic at the wheel!

In a whirlwind of a situation like that, you just stare and feel frightened and numb, and you can't do a thing at first—not till somebody's mind comes to life, which Big Jim's did right then. "We've got to phone the sheriff about the stolen car and tell him there's a baby in the backseat!"

That made sense and brought most of us out of our numb, dumb feeling. One thing was sure. We couldn't do anything with our muscles right now. Even anything we could plan with our *minds,* we couldn't do.

It was Big Jim who went racing toward the house and in to the Thompsons' phone to warn the sheriff about the stolen car and Charlotte Ann in the backseat.

You hear quite a lot about car thieves and how the police give chase, sometimes going a hundred miles an hour. Also sometimes there is shooting from one car to another and terrible accidents in which the people in the runaway car get hurt or even killed.

Big Jim hadn't any sooner gone into the house to make the phone call than he was out again, calling for my mother to give him some information the sheriff had to have—and quick.

I certainly learned something I didn't know about what every car owner ought to keep in his wallet or in a pocket or handbag all the time, so that if his car does get stolen, the police will know what to look for when you call them.

It's not enough to call up and say, "My car was just stolen with my little sister in the backseat! Hurry up and find it for us!"

What the sheriff wanted to know was about nine things: the car's license number, its engine number, its make, model, year, color; did it have any special accessories, any dents, bumps, or noticeable scratches?

That put Mom and her son into more trouble.

"My handbag's in the car!" Mom exclaimed, "and all the papers! Wait, let me talk to him!"

Well, it looked like the Collins family would have to learn a pretty hard lesson about how to be prepared in case their car was ever stolen again.

I was after Mom as fast as I could follow, and I wasn't more than a few feet from her while she told the sheriff—which wasn't the sheriff, anyway, but was his special deputy answering the phone for him—"The car is a four-door, green—"

Mom gave him the license number, which she'd forgotten and I hadn't, and told the sheriff's deputy about the right fender. Our clothesline post had been in the way one day when she was turning around in the yard. The new fender had been put on but wasn't painted yet.

"I left my handbag with all the papers in it in the car!" Mom said. "And my baby's in the backseat!"

Everything that was going on certainly upset the peace and quiet of our day. My heart was as if it had a voice in it saying, "Charlotte Ann—my beautiful little baby sister! Don't let her get hurt! And if I haven't been forgiven for all the things I've done against her that a brother shouldn't, wash that out of my life, too!"

I couldn't tell by the way I *felt* whether my prayer asking forgiveness got answered right then. There was still a heavy feeling in my chest that was terrible—absolutely terrible!

When Mom hung up the phone and for a second her eyes looked into mine, I think I never saw anybody suffering so much.

"It's my fault! I shouldn't have left the key in the ignition," she said.

And then my wonderful mother did something she'd never done before in her whole life. It had always been the other way. From the time I was little, when anything had hurt my heart or some part of my body, I'd gone rushing to her for help, especially when I was very little, like Charlotte Ann. But suddenly my mother came rushing blindly toward *me*. Throwing her arms around me and burying her face against my shoulder, she sobbed. "Oh, Bill! What'll we do! What can we do?"

It was the first time in my life my mother's tears had run down my face. Also it was the first time in my life I'd ever felt she was looking to her son for strength to stand a terrible heartache.

I didn't feel like talking. But I heard my own husky voice answering in her ear that was still against my cheek, "We'll pray, Mother, and God will step in and take charge of things."

It seemed a long time before what I told Mom came true. In fact, it wasn't until quite a while later that day that we found out God really *was* looking out for us and that He was using other people in the neighborhood to help Him do it. He was looking after those other people at the same time.

The phone rang then, two shorts and a long, which I knew was the Thompsons' number. Because I was closer to it than Mrs. Thompson or Poetry, I leaped to answer it, and it was the sheriff's deputy.

"We're setting up roadblocks," he told me, "and we need your help. You boys know where the north road bridge is . . ."

He gave me special orders, which I passed on to the rest of the gang as soon as I could. In a split second we were off, on our way down Poetry's hill to the branch bridge and across it, skirting the edge of a cornfield. At the north road bridge, we piled rails from the fence and stumps and anything else loose and carryable in the road to block the way onto the bridge.

"How come we block the road here?" Little Jim puffed, out of breath from dragging a rail from the other side of the road and plumping it down with the other blockade stuff we were piling there.

"Yeah, how come?" Dragonfly wanted to know, but he was obeying orders without knowing why.

"Because," I told him, repeating in my own words the orders the deputy had given me, "the thugs will see the roadblock the state patrol is putting up two miles up the road beyond your house and may turn back and try to make it across the bridge here and get away. If they do come roaring back and take the north road, *our* blockade'll stop 'em! Hurry up, everybody!"

I got my orders interrupted right then by somebody shouting from the direction of the Till's house. Looking across the bridge, I saw a boy on a bicycle pedaling like mad, steering with one hand and waving with the other and shouting, "Stop! Don't do that! Get that road-block away from there!" And it was Bob Till himself, bareheaded and excited.

What on earth!

I felt my muscles tighten, maybe just from instinct, because the gang had had so much trouble with him and had been forced into so many fights since the first one on Bumblebee Hill.

One thing was for sure: Bob Till wasn't one of the vandals in the stolen car. It also seemed that whatever was on his mind was making him mad. I found out while we were in the middle of the excitement that it was not anger but was something else.

He swung onto the bridge with his bike, pedaled across, and—still ordering us to stop piling up rails and boards and old tree trunks and pieces of stumps—he dived in and started to throw everything back out into the ditch. Some of it rolled down the embankment where it landed against one of the red bridge abutments.

"They'll be here any minute, and we've got to let them through!" he cried. Picking up a long rail the size Abraham Lincoln used to split when he was a little boy, he gave it a heave, grabbed another, and dragged it to the side.

He was hauling away a piece of stump when Big Jim grabbed him. I just knew there was going to be what we'd had before—a rough-and-tumble fight.

But Bob was wiry as well as strong. He twisted out of Big Jim's grasp and cried, "Mother's worse again, and they're sending an ambulance to take her to the hospital! We've got to let them get through!"

That's when I saw, for the first time in my life, tears in Bob Till's eyes. His face, which was shaped quite a lot like his father's face, was worried and looked like any boy's face might look if the boy was scared and needed somebody to help him.

My mind remembered in less than six seconds his mother's face as she had looked when my own mother and I had come into the bedroom where she was, carrying the casserole of food for their supper.

Bob Till's mother might even be dying! We didn't dare block the ambulance from getting through, yet we had to stop the rough boys who had stolen the Collins car with a little girl in it!

In a few seconds we had told Bob what was what and why we were setting up the roadblock.

We had to choose between my mother's hurt, worrying heart and Big Bob Till's mother's life. It seemed, if I could have left the choice up to my own mother, she'd have ordered us, "Tear down that roadblock, boys! Let the ambulance through."

What else my mother might have said if she had had a chance to say anything, I maybe would never know, for right then there was the sound of a car coming at high speed. It had already passed the Collins place and was roaring on to the north road. Would it slow down, I wondered, and make the turn toward the bridge where we were, or would it go racing past to the little branch bridge and up the hill past the Thompson house and toward the other roadblock the deputy said they'd put up farther on?

My question was answered a second later when the Collins family car reached the north road corner, swung right, and came flying down the road to the place where, guarding the bridge, there were seven boys and a still-pretty-good roadblock.

The car's horn was going full blast, ordering us to get out of the way or be killed. The driver, with another boy beside him and with the finest baby sister there ever was in the world somewhere in the back, came roaring like mad toward us.

A terrible thought came to me then: What if the boys were doing more than trying to get away from the police? What if, after they found out Charlotte Ann was in the backseat, they'd decided to kidnap her!

We would find out in less than another minute!

We would have to find out, because the car would have to stop. It just couldn't keep on coming that fast and go crashing into our road-block and on across the bridge.

Before I could finish thinking that, there was a screeching of our car's brakes and a skidding and a fast and furious slowing down.

But it was already too late. Our green car just couldn't stop that quick.

Crash!

The second the bumper and right front

side of the car crashed into the roadblock, Mom's unpainted fender crumpled as if it was a piece of tin. Then the whole car swerved to the right and down the embankment. It stopped when the bumper whammed into the bridge abutment.

There were sounds as well as fast-moving sights, all of them piling up in my mind and exploding. Two car doors were shoved open at the same time, and two boys, one a little bigger than the other, leaped out and started running in different directions—one toward the sycamore tree and the cave and the other toward the fence, which had a few rails missing.

A third boy started running too—Theodore Collins's worried son. I was down that embankment like lightning to find out what if anything had happened to my sister in the backseat—if she was still there.

I quick looked in through the window of the back door and saw her lying upside down on her pink pillow, holding onto her twenty-inch-long panda for dear life, and not a bit hurt.

She was crying, though, and pretty badly scared. But she wasn't crying as hard as she was a minute later when Mom in her blue-flowered dress came running from the Thompsons' house and gathered her up in her arms, crying and exclaiming, "Oh, my poor baby! My poor baby!"

Then my up-to-that-minute brave little sister cut loose with the kind of crying she usually cuts loose with when she's gotten herself hurt and Mom is anywhere around for her to cry to. Most baby girls are like that.

Since Charlotte Ann was safe, I gave excited attention to what else was going on. Big Jim and Circus, being the closest to the shorter boy, had raced after him and already had him down, holding his arms and head to keep from getting hit with hard-knuckled fists or bitten with sharp teeth.

It was the bigger boy that was getting away in spite of Poetry's having tackled him football-style near the rail fence.

Like a streak, that bigger boy was up from the ground and over the fence, headed in the direction of the papaw bushes—with another boy, who was *not* a member of the Sugar Creek Gang, running after him.

That boy who was not a member of the gang and who, ever since he'd moved into the territory, had been our enemy, and who right that minute was streaking off after the runaway vandal, was Big Bob Till!

"Get him down!" Dragonfly called to Bob, when he made a flying leap for the runaway's shoulders. But the vandal shook Bob loose as though he was a smaller boy than he was and raced on.

Now that I knew for sure Charlotte Ann was all right in spite of her noisy crying, there wasn't anything to keep me from joining in the chase. So over the broken-down rail fence I went, trying hard to catch up.

Poetry was puffing along beside and be-hind me.

Things were happening beside the papaw tree, things that I could hear but couldn't see very well until I got there. Two boys were on the ground, with Bob Till on top and using his fists on his man, trying to beat him into giving up.

But the battle changed in another second. The vandal shoved Bob off, then swung around and caught him with a long, hard right to his jaw.

You could hear the impact from as far away as I still was. I saw Bob's knees sag, and he went down, grabbing his opponent's right leg as he fell.

Bob held on for maybe seven feet before he let go. Then he was up and on his own feet again, giving chase as both boys headed for the creek.

Quicker than you could have said, "Jack Robinson," the big rough boy was out into the water, wading and then swimming toward the other side where there was a thicket he could dive into and get away. Also, quicker than you could have said it, Bob was in the water, too. Both boys were in a race to the other side, with Bob not more than nine feet behind.

6

Two boys were in the water, one of them swimming for his life to keep away from a faster-fisted other boy who was also a faster swimmer and gaining inches every second!

My thoughts were pretty well tangled up right that minute. Why in the world would *Bob Till* want to help us capture another boy who was maybe not even as bad a boy as he himself was? Why was he trying to help us at all? He'd been our enemy for so long, how could he all of a sudden want to be our friend?

Even before I could finish asking myself the different questions, it seemed my muddled mind had found the answer. Bob Till was doing it for my mother! She and I had driven all the way over to their house day before yesterday with a hot supper, and Mom had shown that it didn't make any difference in the world that Bob and the Sugar Creek Gang didn't get along.

I could hear Mom's words even now, as every second Bob was gaining on the runaway swimmer, now only four feet ahead of him. "Mrs. Till, we want you to know we love you, and if at any time we can be of help, just let us know."

Also, right that minute, just as Bob made a

lunge forward and grappled with his man, I remembered Mrs. Till's last, sad words before we left: "Pray for my boys!"

It seemed strange at the time, and also right now, that a woman who was so sick that she could hardly talk at all should be thinking about her sons. But maybe that's the way mothers are.

The fight over on the other side of Sugar Creek was up on the shore now and getting pretty fierce. Watching it was sending a shower of shivers up and down my spine. Just when I thought it was over and Bob had won, I saw the vandal, who was on his back at the time with Bob on top of him, double up his legs and kick hard. Both feet landed in Bob's stomach.

Bob Till shot backward toward the creek, stumbled over a pile of drift there from last spring's high water, and landed with an awkward splash in the water under an overhanging willow.

The action was so fast and so surprising, just when I thought the battle was over, that I could hardly believe it. Then the other boy was up and running as fast as he could go. He disappeared into the shrubbery that bordered the creek.

"Bob won't give up!" I heard Poetry exclaim. "He'll be out and after him in a split second."

In a split second he will, I thought. Our old enemy, who was fighting on our side, would come soaking wet out onto the shore and go sloshing like mad into the bushes, giving chase.

But Big Bob Till didn't come sloshing out. Instead, he didn't do anything. I could see from where I was, over on our side of the creek, his blue denim overalls and shirt lying there with a boy in them, right at the edge of the water!

It was Big Jim who all of a sudden realized what had happened. He and Circus had the other boy already tied up, using their handkerchiefs to do it, and he'd come running to see what else was going on and to help if we needed him.

"He—he's knocked out!" he cried excitedly. "We've got to get to him, or he'll drown!"

With that, Big Jim—our fuzzy-mustached leader, whose muscles, like the village blacksmith's, were as strong as iron bands and who had been the one of our gang that Bob Till hated the most— Big Jim kicked off his hiking shoes and in a few fast-flying seconds was down the embankment and into the water, wading and swimming, hurrying across Sugar Creek as fast as he could to see if he could help his enemy stay alive!

It really wasn't the time when a boy would ordinarily be thinking of something he had read in the leather-bound Bible that lies on the library table near a cracked mirror. But a thought came to my mind, and it was: "Greater love has no one than this, that one lay down his life for his friends." And I knew Who had done it first!

Along with the verse, while Big Jim was still splashing his way across, was the memory of the time in Chicago when Bob had needed a blood transfusion to save his life, and Big Jim had volunteered some of his. You'd think that any boy who had quite a lot of a good boy's blood in him wouldn't keep on having such a wicked heart, but that hadn't seemed to make any difference with Bob. He had kept right on being ornery.

Now other things were going on at the bridge. Turning north at the corner by the Collins family's orchard was a long, gray ambulance, coming fast to go over the bridge to the Tills' house to get Mrs. Till and take her to the hospital.

The ambulance hadn't any sooner stopped —they had to take out of the way a few rails from a fence and a piece or two of an old stump—than there was a yell from under the overhanging willow where Big Jim had just pulled Bob out of the water. "Help! Somebody! He's drowned! We've got to give him artificial respiration!"

And now the ambulance driver would have to make a decision: whether to drive on over to the Tills' house for Bob's mother or cross the bridge, stop, jump out of the ambulance, and go racing down to where Big Jim was and give artificial respiration to her son!

It seemed I knew that if Bob Till's very sick mother was there and had a chance to say what to do, she'd say with her sick, sad voice, "Save my boy! I've already lived half of my life, and he's just beginning!"

It wasn't easy for the men in the ambulance to decide, but I knew they would decide at least to rush down to see if Bob actually was drowned before going on to get his mother. And that is what they did.

A little later, I was across the bridge and down past the washed-clean abutment and at the place where the resuscitation was going on. Those of us who weren't helping were in a little circle, just watching.

Things were moving fast. The two men from the ambulance were working as though they'd done things like this before. First, they wiped out Bob's mouth to be sure there wasn't any sand or pickerel weed in it from the creek. Then, with Bob lying on his back, they tilted his head back until his chin was pointing upward. "Get the jaw in a jutting-out position," I heard one of the men say, "so the base of his tongue won't obstruct the airway."

As best I could, without getting in the way, I watched them working to save Bob, whose face was pasty pale.

One of the men was on his knees at Bob's head now. With his mouth opened wide, he placed it tightly over Bob's, one hand holding Bob's nose shut.

"What's he doing that for?" Dragonfly asked me.

Little Jim said, "He's blowing air into his lungs!" which a second later, I knew was the truth. The man who'd just done the blowing put his left ear to Bob's mouth to listen and find out if any of the air he'd just blown in came out again.

"They do it and keep on doing it till he can breathe by himself," Little Jim explained.

Three times, the dark-haired ambulance driver blew, and three times he listened, and three times he didn't hear any air coming back out.

"There's an obstruction!" he said grimly. "We've got to get it out, whatever it is."

Action speeded up then, and a great big lump of fear came from somewhere and landed in my heart and stayed there. All the mean things Bob Till had ever done to us or said about us, all the hard-knuckled fists he had landed on Big Jim's nose in the Battle of Bumblebee Hill, plus all the other things—it seemed I wanted to forgive every one of them and have my thoughts about him be as pure as God had made my heart that very afternoon when I'd been on my knees beside the library table near the cracked mirror.

I didn't pray out loud, but God could hear me anyway. There was a heavy ache in my heart, and it was crying and saying, "Please, heavenly Father, don't let Bob Till die! Spare him and make him a Christian. Give him time to become one before You let him die!"

Quicker than a flash, the gray-haired ambulance man turned Bob to his side and gave him three or four sharp blows between the shoulder blades, saying to the dark-haired man, "We've got to dislodge whatever is obstructing."

Again they had Bob on his back, his chin tilted up and forward, and again the dark-haired man was blowing and listening, blowing and listening, blowing and listening . . .

"He's coming to! I hear it! Air is coming back!"

If I had known at the time as much as I knew later, I could have guessed Bob would be breathing again in a few minutes—or even in a few seconds—because I'd noticed a little twitching of his fingers, and once I thought I heard him give a sighlike gasp.

It certainly was different from the easy way the different members of the gang had come back to life when we had practiced the prone resuscitation method on ourselves. We wouldn't any sooner start breathing again than we'd roll over from our face-down position and be on our feet, feeling fine in a few seconds and ready for a footrace with somebody.

Pretty soon Bob was fully conscious and trying to sit up but not being allowed to. He wasn't strong enough to, anyway.

Explaining it later, the gray-haired man said, "Every drowning case should be treated as a potential case of shock, and we usually take them to the hospital for a while."

Bob, still not being allowed to sit up, all of a sudden asked, "Where's my mother? What happened? Where's the—"

I knew he was now remembering the fight he had been in and the vandal who had gotten away. His face was still pasty white, but there was a touch of color beginning to show in his cheeks, and I was glad. I tell you, glad!

But life had to go on. The ambulance would have to go on to Bob's house, and we all would start in living again where we'd left off. Everything had happened so fast that it seemed only half an hour had gone by. What an afternoon it had been, and it wasn't over yet!

Just then, from across the creek and the woods, there came the startling wail of a police siren, and almost before I could turn around to look, there the patrol car was, away up on the north road and headed for the bridge.

I tell you there was excitement for a while, although it wasn't the kind of nervous excitement we'd been having, because Charlotte Ann was all right, Bob Till's life had been saved, and the terrible ache in my heart was gone.

It took two policemen from the patrol car only a few seconds to get across the bridge and down the embankment and the hundred yards up the shore to where we all were. Bob Till, still not feeling full of pep, was coughing a little now on account of the water he'd had in his stomach and lungs.

Then Dragonfly spotted something on the ground at the edge of the creek. He made a dive for it, scooped it up, and shoved it into his jeans pocket. His movements were so fast that I didn't get to see what it was, and I supposed it maybe didn't matter anyway.

But it did matter. We found that out when the police began asking a lot of questions.

They searched all over the place for any clues that might help them identify the runaway vandal when and if they captured him. "Any of you boys find anything here that'll help us?" they asked, and not a one of us said we had.

"I'll know him if I see him again!" Bob Till, still pale and weak, said.

Several of the rest of us said the same thing.

Dragonfly made me angry when *he* said, "Who gets the reward money if we identify him?"

"Honestly!" Poetry squawked and scowled fiercely at our pop-eyed gang member.

I hadn't planned to do what I did right then. But quicker than a chick's chirp, I swung around toward that greedy rascal, shoved my hand into his jeans pocket, and pulled out—of all things in the world—a piece of wet gray cloth about four inches square.

Well, that little crooked-nosed guy flew into a temper tantrum and struggled all around me, trying to get it back.

Holding Dragonfly at arms' length, I held out the piece of gray cloth and said to the police, "Here's the only clue we've found so far."

Bob Till's eyes focused on the piece of cloth while the officer studied it. "That," Bob said, "is his shirt pocket. I felt it come off in my hand while we were still in the water. I must have held onto it without knowing it."

And that was that. The ambulance drivers took Mrs. Till and Bob to the hospital. The police got going in their search for the missing vandal, whose partner we'd already caught and tied up there by the bridge. And a tow truck was called to come and pull the Collins family car backward out of the ditch, where its front bumper rested against the bridge abutment.

What a lot of excitement there had been! More in the last few days than a boy could expect to have in one whole summer or even in a year! It was hard to believe it had all happened to us, and right in our own neighborhood.

I was chewing it all over in my mind one day about a week later, while I was out in the garden with the Golden Bantam sweet corn, the black-seeded Simpson lettuce, and the Ebenezer onions.

My father, who had been standing near the iron pitcher pump where our car was parked, admiring his new paint job on the second right front fender we had had put on that summer, took a final look at it and came out to the garden gate. There he raised his right arm to wipe the sweat from his forehead, using his shirt sleeve to do it because he had a paint spray gun in one hand and paint spatters on the other. Also, that shirt sleeve was about the only place left on everything he was wearing that didn't have paint on it.

I was feeling especially fine. Today was the day Bob Till's mother was coming home from the hospital. She'd had her operation the same day the ambulance took her and was making what they called a "good recovery."

"Son?" my father said to me with a question mark on the end of his voice.

"Yes sir?" I answered him with a question mark on mine.

"The boys of the Sugar Creek Gang are growing up. Do you know that?"

I stopped my hand plow and straightened to my full height. Dad's tone of voice made me feel four or five inches taller. My own voice sounded like a young rooster learning to crow as I answered, "Do we have to? Can't we just keep on being boys?"

For some reason, as much as I wanted to be older and bigger, the idea of growing up seemed like saying good-bye to the very wonderful boys' world I'd been living in. It might even mean the scattering of the Sugar Creek Gang, which would be about the worst thing that could ever happen to me.

"You have to, and you can't," Dad answered. Then he explained. "Part of growing up is learning to do things for others, sacrificing for somebody else. All the rest of your lives, you boys will be proud of yourselves—in the right way, I mean—for refusing the hundred-dollar reward for the capture of those vandals.

Your turning it over to Bob for his mother's hospital and doctor expenses was one of the most unselfish things you could ever have done."

"But *we* didn't deserve the money," I said. "Only half of it. We caught only one of them. And even if Bob didn't capture the other one but the police did, the pocket he tore off the other boy's shirt in the fight was lying right there beside him when he came to after almost drowning. The reward was for evidence leading to the capture of the vandals—and that shirt pocket was part of the evidence."

That was another thing I had been chewing over in my mind— how even that little torn-off shirt pocket had had a share in helping the police. When they had captured a scared teenager over on the other side of Wolf Creek not far from the church, he had had a missing shirt pocket.

Dad answered me with what at first sounded like a riddle. He said with a grin in his voice, "It looks like the worm has turned at Sugar Creek."

"Worm?" I took a quick look down at where I had been cultivating to see if any big fat fish worm down there might be twisting and turning as a fish worm does when it gets plowed up. But there wasn't a single worm in sight.

"I mean," Dad explained, "that Bob Till used to be your enemy. Now, all of a sudden he is your friend. It's just an expression," he added. "People say that when a situation is reversed. But how," he went on to ask, "can you boys get along without having somebody to stir up trouble for you now and then?"

"Oh, we'll manage. We still have Shorty Long," I said, remembering the new boy who a while back had moved into the neighborhood and upset the peace and quiet of the whole territory with the kind of trouble most everybody knows about in the exciting story called *The Blue Cow*. "He's on his vacation now, but he'll be back next week sometime."

But Dad was right. The worm *had* turned at Sugar Creek. We probably never again would have any trouble with Big Bob Till.

"One thing I'd like to know," I called from the other end of an onion row, "is what you and Mom are going to do about whether to spank or not to spank."

There was a twinkle in Dad's eyes as he growled out his answer from under his reddish brown mustache, "Oh—that! We're going to do it your mother's way when I'm away from home, and my way when I'm here!"

"Don't I get to have anything to say about which way?" I asked. There was such a good feeling between us at the time that it seemed all right to ask the question.

Dad's answer was a little puzzling. "Your way, of course, is just to take it whichever way it happens to be given. You understand, don't you, why your mother can't punish you corporally?"

"Corporally?" I had never before heard the word used in our family.

Dad waved his spray gun, pressed the trigger, and a foggy stream of green paint came out its nozzle. Then he explained, "Your mother has a very tender heart, Son. She just can't stand to hurt you bodily. That's what 'corporally' means—'bodily.'"

"Is a boy's stomach part of his body?" I asked with a grin in my voice, thinking I had just thought of a good joke and could hardly wait for Dad's yes answer.

When he said a stomach was, I asked, "Then, when a boy gets hunger pangs from missing out on a piece of custard pie, couldn't you call that corporal punishment?"

Dad grinned as if the joke was only partly humorous, but he winked at me as he said, "We could call it that, but . . . well . . . suppose we don't."

"Also," I went on, now a little more seriously, "what could be harder on a boy's legs and arms, which are part of his body, than to wear out their muscles pushing a cultivator on a sultry afternoon?"

"One thing is for sure," Dad changed his tone of voice to say, "your mother's punishment was the right kind for you last week while I was away." He came through the gate then, set his spray gun on the flat top of one of the gateposts, wiped his hands on a piece of a boy's worn-out shirt he had pulled from one of his pockets, picked up a hoe, and began to chop away at some small pigweeds growing in the now almost knee-high Golden Bantam.

"It took quite a lot of valuable fishing time," I disagreed in a friendly voice, pushing my plow along in the hot sunlight. "And sometimes it's good for a boy to make up for lost time even if it's a whole week later," I finished hopefully.

But Dad wasn't that kind of hopeful. Here is his explanation as to why my having to work several hours in the garden last week was better punishment than the beech switch kind—for that day, anyway.

"In the first place, it took a lot longer," he said. "Which meant you got a lot of garden work done. In the second place, it kept you here long enough so you could answer the phone when Leslie called from Old Man Paddler's. And it all worked out for the very best to help you capture the vandals and even to save Bob's life. Everything would have worked out in a different way if you'd been given what you call your fast, noisy punishment and you'd gone with the gang."

It made sense. Things had had to be just as they had been.

A question came into my mind then, one I kind of wanted to ask Dad. But even though both of us believed the same way about the Bible, it wasn't easy to talk to him about it, maybe because he was a lot older. It seemed it was easier to talk to Little Jim about things like that than to anybody else. So I just swallowed my curiosity.

But later that afternoon, after Dad was

gone to town and Dragonfly came over to see if I had time to goof around with him a while, I got the answer I wanted. In fact, I answered the question myself.

"It's this way," I explained to Dragonfly, "if I hadn't been home working that afternoon, I'd have missed Poetry's phone call. If I'd missed it, I wouldn't have been at the cave when the vandals came charging out and wouldn't have known which way they went. I wouldn't have been there to give the sheriff's deputy the news on the phone and gotten his orders to set up the roadblock. Bob wouldn't have seen us doing it and come to stop us. He wouldn't have gotten into the fight with the boy that tried to get away. And we wouldn't have had the shirt pocket you found as evidence. It's just like it says in the Bible."

Then I quoted to Dragonfly, whose folks hadn't taught him very much about the Bible, a very special verse I had memorized at family devotions: "And we know that God causes all things to work together for good to those who love God, to those who are called according to His purpose."

I was still with the Ebenezer onions, and Dragonfly was chopping around a little with the weeding hoe. He raised the hoe high then and brought it down with a savage slice at a weed that was too small for corporal punishment and said, "Weeds don't work together for good—not that one, anyway."

"Maybe they do." I was surprised I was

smart enough to say that. "Maybe if there weren't any weeds at all, we wouldn't cultivate the garden as much as we should and wouldn't get as good a crop."

It seemed we had talked about that long enough, and pretty soon he said, "Bob Till came over to our house this morning, and look what he gave me!"

Dragonfly turned his back and leaned over to show me a brand-new gray patch his mother had sewed on his pants.

"What do you mean, what he gave you?" I asked.

"Shirt pocket," he said with a grin. "Bob said I could keep it for a souvenir, and Mom made a patch out of it for my pants that got torn when I climbed through the fence to get down to where he was getting worked on."

The phone in our house rang then, two long longs and a short short, and in a minute Mom was at the back door calling, "It's your mother, Roy. She wants you to come home and help with the garden work!"

And then I was alone again. My father was away, and I was sweating and grunting along, pushing the cultivator and wishing I could be doing something else. And that's when it happened again. Right in front of my eyes I turned up with my plow shovel six or seven of the largest, juiciest-looking, wriggling, lively fishing worms anybody ever saw!

I stopped and stood and stared at them while they stretched themselves out and inched their way along, trying to get back into the ground.

Then I said, "Oh, no, you don't! Maybe if I put you on a hook away down under the water, you'd bring up a sunfish or a bass. But my father, who handles the beech switches, would rather you'd go back down into the ground, eat as much garden soil down there as you can stuff yourselves with, and come back up tonight with what you couldn't digest and deposit it right here on the surface where the Ebenezer onions can get at it!"

Later that afternoon—in fact, it was getting close to chore time—I went out into the barn and up into the haymow and lay down in the sweet-smelling alfalfa, having ordered myself to take a short rest.

There my eyes roamed around, resting on different things—the long beam I sometimes used for a platform for Lincoln's Gettysburg Address, the wooden box I'd made and placed away up on a mantel-like shelf for pigeons to nest in, the net hanging from the iron hoop we used for basketball practice, and the sparrow's nest on another log, which I'd have to tear out sometime. Then I closed my eyes to see what, if anything, would flash upon my inner eye.

And do you know what? It wasn't at all like what somebody named Wordsworth had had flash on *his* inner eye. It was, instead, a host of Golden Bantam sweet corn with its blades tossing in the breeze, and its husky, rusty rustle was calling me to get up and come and do something about the weeds that were growing between the rows.

The *Sugar Creek Gang* Series: